Fiona
Finds Her Tongue

Diana Hendry

Illustrated by Victoria Cooper

Puffin Books

for Kate

Puffin Books, Penguin Books Ltd, Harmondsworth, Middlesex, England
Viking Penguin Inc., 40 West 23rd Street, New York, New York 10010, U.S.A.
Penguin Books Australia Ltd, Ringwood, Victoria, Australia
Penguin Books Canada Ltd, 2801 John Street, Markham, Ontario, Canada L3R 1B4
Penguin Books (N.Z.) Ltd, 182–190 Wairau Road, Auckland 10, New Zealand

First published by Julia MacRae Books, a division of Franklin Watts Ltd 1985
Published in Puffin Books 1987

Copyright © Diana Hendry, 1985
Illustrations copyright © Victoria Cooper, 1985
All rights reserved

Printed and bound in Great Britain by
Cox & Wyman Ltd, Reading
Typeset in Plantin

Chapter 1

At home Fiona talked and talked
and talked and talked.

She talked to her panda, Elias,
when she woke up in the morning.
She talked to her shoes that stood by
the cupboard.

"I'm coming soon shoes," said
Fiona, snuggling down under the
blankets.

She talked to the radiator and the radiator talked back. It gurgled and grumbled and groaned about all the hard work it had to do making the house warm.

Fiona talked to her mother at breakfast. All through mouthfuls of crunchy Ricicles and toast Fiona talked. She talked to the dog, Stew-pot, and she talked to the cat, Sprogs.

"Stew-pot, you are not having any of my crusts this morning," Fiona would say, "I'm hungry."

And to Sprogs: "Don't you think Ricicles are much nicer than fish fingers, Sprogs?" (But Sprogs stretched a lazy paw and stalked away. He thought it was a silly question.)

And when there was nothing and nobody to talk to, Fiona talked to herself. She talked to herself all the way upstairs to the bathroom. She talked to herself in the mirror. "Well, well, don't you look a mess this morning!" she said to Fiona-in-the-mirror. "What big eyes you have and what big teeth!" and she stuck

her teeth out like the fangs of the
wolf in Little Red Riding Hood.

When Fiona's father came home
from work, Fiona rushed to the gate
to meet him. And she talked. All the
way up the garden path, all the way
into the kitchen and all the way up
the stairs. Fiona's father shut
himself in the bathroom. Fiona sat
outside. And talked.

"She never stops!" said Fiona's
mother. "She's more than a
chatter-box. She's a gibble-gabble!
She's a wind-bag! She's like my
seven-day alarm clock! Do you
know she even talks in her sleep?"
And it was true. Fiona did.

But Fiona did all her talking at

home. Outside of Number 21 Victoria Drive, Crouch End, something funny happened to Fiona. She stopped talking. When she went to the shops with her mother, when she

went to birthday parties, when she went to tea with her grandma, when she went to visit the doctor or the dentist, Fiona said . . . nothing.

"Are you going to carry the potatoes for your mum?" asked the vegetable shop lady, and Fiona would clutch the bag of potatoes to her chest and say . . . nothing.

"Isn't she a shy little thing!" said the lady.

"Would you like banana sand-wiches or tomato?" Fiona was asked when she went to a birthday party. And Fiona would try very hard to say, "I would love a banana sandwich and I'd hate a tomato sandwich because of all the slimey, squelchy pips." But nothing would come out. Not even, "Banana, please." At almost every party Fiona ate tomato-and-slimey-pips sandwiches.

"How is my little Fiona today?" her grandma would ask when Fiona and her mother arrived for tea. And Fiona wanted to say, "I'm horrid and cross today and I've got a big scratch on my arm and Daddy won't let me have dancing lessons and Mummy made me wear this ugghy

green T-shirt and I HATE it."

But she said nothing of this. She just hid her face against her mother's arm and giggled.

"Don't be silly, Fiona," said her mother, "you're not a baby."

And Grandma said what Grandma always said: "Oh, Fiona's lost her tongue again."

Now Fiona knew perfectly well that she had not lost her tongue because when Grandma had first said this, she had gone to the mirror in the hall and looked. Her tongue was still there, popping in and out of her mouth like a little pink Punch from Punch and Judy.

But *something* happened to her tongue. It seemed to get very fat and take up all the space in her mouth. It seemed to get jammed between her teeth like a car in a too-tight car-parking place. It curled up inside her mouth (like Stew-pot in his basket when he'd been bad and was scared) and it wouldn't wag.

"Whatever will you do when you

go to school?" asked Grandma.

"I really don't know," sighed
Fiona's mother, answering for
Fiona. And nor did Fiona. Fiona
cried about it at night, in bed. She
was to start school in a week's time.
The teacher would ask her questions.
She would expect Fiona to answer
them. Other children would talk to
her. Would *they* think she had lost
her tongue too?

"Whatever is the matter?" asked
Fiona's father when he found her
curled up in bed making Elias
soggy with tears.

"I can't talk!" sobbed Fiona.
"How can I go to school if I can't
talk? And Grandma says I've lost

my tongue. Only I haven't. It's right there inside my mouth (and Fiona stuck it out), but it's so crowded with words in there that not one of them can wriggle out."

"Plenty are coming out now!" said her father, stroking Fiona's hair which some called ginger and some called red and some called auburn.

"But that's at home!" wailed Fiona. "My tongue is happy here, it wags quite easily. See (and Fiona wagged), it's no trouble at all at home!"

"I have noticed!" said her father, laughing. "Fiona, do you know what I think is the matter with your tongue?"

"What?" asked Fiona.

"Your tongue is like a tap when you turn it on too hard," said her father. "All the water – or the words – come rushing out. Sometimes, when a lot of water has built up in the tank and you turn the tap on, nothing happens. It gives a cough

and a splutter and stops. It's so full
up with water it can't make a start.
Have you noticed?"

"Yes, I have," said Fiona. "My
tank has built up such a lot of words
inside it that I can't get started
either."

"I know," said her father. "I've
never known a bigger tank of words
in all my life. Listen, tomorrow let's
try an experiment. When you are at
home just turn your word-tap on a
little bit. Say a few words at a time.
Then have a rest. Try a little
silence, Fiona."

Fiona stared at her father in
amazement. "And you think that
will work? You think that will get

my tongue to wag the way it ought to wag?"

"I think it very well might," said her father, tucking her in.

"I'll try it!" said Fiona and she folded her lips tight as if she was practising silence.

Chapter 2

The next morning Fiona did not talk to Elias and she did not talk to her shoes (although she gave them a wave so that they would know they were not forgotten).

At breakfast she was just about to tell her mother what an odd thing it was that her radiator not only gurgled and grumbled and groaned at her, but it also WINKED! The early morning light rippled along the ridges of the radiator and the radiator winked. Now wasn't that odd? And Fiona tried to wink back but it was very difficult because . . .

Fiona was about to say all this but then she stopped. She had caught her father's eye. Her father grinned and put his finger to his lips in a 'Ssshhh' sort of way.

Fiona took a big gulp of air,

turned her tap of words until it was just going ker-plop-plop-plop, and said, very carefully, "My radiator winked at me this morning."

"How do you mean, winked?" asked Fiona's mother. She suspected a joke.

Fiona took another gulp of air and turned her tap on just a little bit more. "All its crinkly edges went glint, glint, glint," said Fiona and skidded to a full stop the way Stew-pot did when he rushed down the stairs too fast and met the front door.

"Oh I *see*!" said her mother at once. "As *if* it was winking."

Fiona nodded. (Today she wasn't

even going to waste a 'yes'.)

Fiona's father, ready for work, kissed the top of her head and whispered, "Well done!"

For the rest of the morning it was very quiet at 21 Victoria Drive, Crouch End. "Do you feel all right?" Fiona's mother asked her. "You're very quiet today."

"I'm looking after the tap," said Fiona.

"That's nice, dear," said her mother who was busy making a cake for Grandma.

Fiona wanted to say that it wasn't
at all nice and however did Stew-pot
and Sprogs and the flowers in the
garden manage without words?
But she didn't. Perhaps, thought
Fiona, people were born with
different kinds of word-taps like
they had different types of noses.

When she had made the cake,
Fiona's mother called Fiona
upstairs.

"I want you to practise tying your
shoe-laces for school," said her
mother.

They sat on the floor together and
Fiona's mother made a loop of lace.

"That's the tree trunk," said
Fiona's mother.

Fiona said nothing.

Her mother made a loop of the second lace.

"That's the rabbit," she said.

Still Fiona said nothing.

"And here goes the rabbit round the tree trunk and up the hole under the tree," said Fiona's mother. "And there's the bow!" And she pulled the two laces tight in a nice, neat bow.

Now there were a great many things Fiona wanted to say about the rabbit and the tree. How, she wanted to ask, was she to know which lace was the rabbit and which the tree? Could she colour the laces, perhaps, with her Pentels. One

lace green and one lace yellow, and then she would remember. She wanted to say that a shoe lace made a very skinny rabbit. She wanted to ask if the bow, when it was made, was meant to be the rabbit's ears popping out of the hole.

Fiona practised silence for such a long time that her mother felt her forehead to see if she was getting chickenpox like Alice-down-the-road.

At last Fiona turned her word-tap to allow just the tiniest drip. "Rabbit's ears!" said Fiona.

"What?" asked her mother, startled.

Fiona pointed to the bow and said again, "Rabbit's ears."

"Oh I *see*," said her mother. "The bow looks like the rabbit's ears sticking out of the hole. Well you have a practice while I get things ready to go to Grandma's."

What a lot of practising, thought Fiona, but she sat on the floor and made the rabbit shoe lace run round the tree shoe lace. She didn't talk to the rabbit. She didn't talk to the tree. She didn't talk to her shoes and she didn't talk to herself. And there was no fun in it. It was very dull.

By the time Fiona's mother was ready for Grandma's, there were so many words in Fiona's word tank that she thought she might burst. The words gurgled and groaned and grumbled inside her just like the hot water in the radiator getting hotter and wanting to rush through the pipes.

Fiona's mother walked slowly. She

did not want to shake the chocolate cake in its tin. At last Grandma's house was in sight! Fiona could bear it no longer. She rushed up the path, burst in the back door and she opened her mouth to let all those lovely warm words go running about Grandma's house.

Fiona was about to say: "Grandma! Grandma! I'm going to school tomorrow! I can tie my own shoe laces and make the rabbit run round the tree. And Alice-down-the-road has got chickenpox."

That is what Fiona *wanted* to say. But then the awful thing happened. She opened her mouth and nothing came out. Not a word. Her tongue was in a traffic jam between her teeth. Her cheeks went scarlet. Tears came to her eyes.

"Oh dear," said Grandma, as Grandma *always* said, "Fiona's lost her tongue again." And then Fiona's tank did burst, not into words, but tears.

"I think Fiona is a bit upset today," said her mother, arriving with the chocolate cake safe in its tin. "She starts school tomorrow, you know."

"I know," said Grandma. "I've bought her a present." And she went to the cupboard under the stairs where she kept her surprises, and she brought out a large square parcel wrapped in green tissue paper with a big gold ribbon tied in a rabbit's ears bow.

When Fiona opened it she found it was a scarlet leather school satchel with shining silver buckles and a little see-through pocket in the front where she could write her name and address.

"Ooooh, Grandma!" cried Fiona, forgetting all about taps and tanks and silences. "It's the most beautiful satchel I've ever seen!"

And Grandma laughed and said, "Just listen! Fiona's found her tongue!"

Then Fiona blushed as red as her hair and lost her tongue all over again!

"Oh," cried Fiona to her father when she and her tongue were safely home again and he was sitting on the edge of her bed at bed-time. "However am I going to get my taps just right?"

"I think you've made a very good start," said her father. "After all, you did manage to say *something* to Grandma and Mummy tells me you've practised a lot of silence at home."

"But it's the Off, On, Off, On, part I can't manage," said Fiona. "What will happen at school if my word tap is Off when it should be On and On when it should be Off?"

Fiona's father thought for a moment.

"Listen," he said, "I've got a

magic little something that I'm going to put in your satchel so that you can use it if you really get stuck for words. Right?"

"Right," said Fiona.

Then her father wrote something on a piece of paper and 'posted' it in the pocket of Fiona's satchel.

Fiona fell asleep and dreamt that her satchel was a talking satchel and whenever the teacher asked her a question the satchel answered for her.

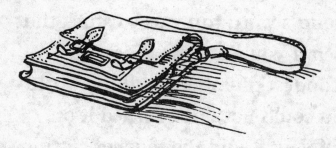

Chapter 3

But of course the satchel didn't say a word.

And nor did Fiona!

On that first morning at school Fiona's word tap was so stuck that even if you were the biggest, strongest plumber in all the world you could not have turned it on.

"Now," said the teacher, sitting

at her desk, "every morning I take the register. That means I have a list of your names here and I read them out and when I call *your* name, you say, 'Yes Miss'. That's so I know you are all here and nobody's missing. We'll do it slowly this morning so that I can get to know all your names." And off she went:—

Amanda? Yes, Miss ✓ (whisper)
Thomas ? Yes, Miss ✓ (giggle-and-squeak)
Jane ? Yes, Miss ✓ (loud-and-brave)
Rowena? Yes, Miss ✓ (pianissimo)
David? Yes, Miss ✓ (dolce)
Fiona ?

"FIONA? FIONA? FIONA?"
Fiona's name seemed to echo
round the classroom like a bit of
'hot' running all round the pipes.
Fiona dug frantically in her satchel
for her father's magic-something,
for if ever a magic-something was
needed, now was the moment. She
pulled out the piece of paper. Her
father had drawn a picture of Fiona
and in the picture Fiona wore an
enormous smile. At once Fiona

smiled. She smiled so wide she thought she'd come to the end of her cheeks. The teacher looked up and saw her. "Oh there you are, Fiona," she said. "I expect you've lost your tongue this morning. We all feel rather shy on the first day."

There were twenty-four children in Fiona's class and twenty-two of them said, "Yes, Miss."

"Tai?" called the teacher, ticking her way down the register, "Tai?" And there was a silence just like Fiona's silence only when Fiona looked round to see who owned this silence, she saw that Tai didn't have a red satchel with a magic-something in it and Tai's silence wasn't a smiling silence, it was a sad silence. Two tears were about to slide down his nose.

But the teacher saw Tai's tears
just as she had seen Fiona's smile.
"Well, children," said the teacher,
"this is Tai. He comes all the way
from Vietnam so I don't suppose he
knows much English yet. We must
all try to help him."

Fiona looked at Tai in horror. *She*
knew what it was like to lose her
tongue, to be stuck for words. But to
have an empty word tank or a tank
full of words that nobody else could
understand . . . well! Not one word,
not twenty words, could say how
awful that must be.

For the first lesson the children
were to do some painting. Fiona
took a palette of paints from the

cupboard over to the table which
the teacher had spread with
newspapers and set out with yoghurt
pots full of water. There were lots of
brushes standing in jam-jars like
bunches of hairy flowers.

Fiona found herself sitting next to
Tai.

"I want you all to paint me a
picture of your own house," said the
teacher, "with the garden if you
want to."

Fiona took a pencil and began to
draw 21 Victoria Drive, Crouch End.
She drew a square, four crooked
windows (with Sprogs in one of
them), a door with a very big
letter-box and a garden path lined

with speechless flowers.

Tai stared at his empty piece of paper. It was as empty as his word tank. All he could colour it with was two more tears.

And then, as if someone had applied just a very little oil to the stiff washers of Fiona's word-tap, Fiona found her tongue.

"House!" said Fiona to Tai,

pointing to her own picture.
"House!" she said again. Tai
looked at her. He had a fringe of
silky black hair and eyes that shone
like the glossy school piano in the
big hall.

"Owss?" said Tai.

"House!" said Fiona.

"Owss!" said Tai. But he picked
up his pencil and began to draw.

But Tai did not draw a house. He
drew a boat.

"No," said Fiona, pointing to his
picture. "Boat. Not house. Boat."
And then pointing from his picture
to her picture, "Boat, house, boat,
house."

"But, owss, but, owss," said Tai

and they both giggled so much that the teacher came to see what was going on.

When she saw Tai's picture of a boat she said, "I expect Tai's home has been a boat. You see, when there was a war, Tai's family lost their house and they spent months and months sailing to England in a boat. I expect a boat means home to Tai."

"But!" said Tai, spotting this one word out of all the others the teacher had used.

The teacher laughed. "Oh well done, Tai! You're learning English fast. Thank you for being so helpful, Fiona."

But Tai was busy drawing as fast as he could. He drew four windows, a door and a chimney. "Owss!" said Tai, beaming and pointing to the new picture. And, "But!" said Tai pointing to the first picture.

"This is a house," said Fiona, pointing to Tai's 'owss', "BUT this is a boat," pointing to Tai's 'but'.

"But," said Tai.

"Boat," said Fiona and they both burst out laughing again.

And after that Fiona's word-tap went Off and On just when she

wanted it to and by the time Tai
went home to his 'owss' he had four
new English words and one new
English friend. The words were
HOUSE (owss), BOAT (but), YES
(yuss), NO (nuh) and the friend, of
course, was Fiona (Nona).

When Fiona's father came home
from work that evening, Fiona
rushed down the garden to meet
him. "Daddy, it was all right!" cried
Fiona. "My tap worked! I thought it
was stuck for ever but then I met
Tai and Tai didn't have any words

at all so I had to give him some from my word tank. And now he's got four new words!"

"So I suppose you didn't need the magic-something in your satchel after all?" said her father.

"Oh Daddy, I did, I did. Right at the beginning, when I wanted to say 'Yes, Miss' and nothing would come out. *Then* I needed it."

"Did it work?" asked her father.

"It did!" said Fiona. "Miss knew at once who I was without my saying a word."

"You don't always need words," said Fiona's father.

"No," agreed Fiona, "but they're nice to have around, aren't they?"

"And so are you!" said her father giving her a hug.

"I know another magic something," said Fiona, "something just as magic as smiles."

"What's that?" asked her father.

"Tears," said Fiona. Then her father took her hand and they walked up the path together without saying a word. And that was a magic silence.

ONE NIL
Tony Bradman

Dave Brown is mad about football, and when he learns that
the England squad are to train at the local City ground he
thinks up a brilliant plan to overcome his parents' objections
and gets to the ground to see them. A very amusing story.

THE GHOST AT No. 13
Gyles Brandreth

Hamlet Brown's sister, Susan, is just too perfect. Everything
she does is praised and Hamlet is in despair – until the ghost
comes to stay for a holiday and helps him to find an exciting
idea for his school project.

ZOZU THE ROBOT
Diana Carter

Rufus and Sarah find a tiny frightened little robot and his
space capsule in their garden.

SEE YOU AT THE MATCH
Margaret Joy

Six delightful stories about football. Whether spectator, player, winner or loser, these short, easy stories for young readers are a must for all football fans.

RAGDOLLY ANNA'S CIRCUS
Jean Kenward

Made only from a morsel of this and a tatter of that, Ragdolly Anna is a very special doll. These adventures of the popular doll are based on the television series.

CHRIS AND THE DRAGON
Fay Sampson

Chris is always in trouble of one kind or another, but does try extra hard to be good when he is chosen to play Joseph in the school nativity play. This hilarious story ends with a glorious celebration of the Chinese New Year.

RADIO ALERT RADIO DETECTIVE
John Escott

Two exciting stories centred around a local radio station, Roundbay Radio. There's a mystery in each book which the children involved help to solve brilliantly.

TALES FROM ALLOTMENT LANE SCHOOL
Margaret Joy

Twelve delightful stories, bright, light and funny, about the children in Miss Mee's class at Allotment Lane School. Meet Ian, the avid collector, Mary and Gary who have busy mornings taking messages, and school caterpillars who disappear and turn up again in surprising circumstances.

THE THREE AND MANY WISHES OF JASON REID
Hazel Hutchins

Jason is eleven and a very good thinker so when he is granted three wishes he is very wary indeed. After all, he knows the tangles that happen in fairy stories!

HANK PRANK AND HOT HENRIETTA
Jules Older

Hank and his hot-tempered sister, Henrietta, are always getting themselves into trouble but the doings of this terrible pair make for an entertaining series of adventures.

THE AIR-RAID SHELTER
Jeremy Strong

Adam and his sister Rachel find a perfect place for their secret camp in the grounds of a deserted house, until they are discovered by their sworn enemies, the Bradley boys, and things just go from bad to worse.

ELOISE
Kay Thompson

At the Plaza Hotel, surrounded by her dog, her turtle, her nanny and a host of hotel guests, six-year-old Eloise is never bored . . .

THE CONKER AS HARD AS A DIAMOND
Chris Powling

Little Alpesh's burning ambition is to find a diamond-hard conker, to make his champion of the universe! A zany tale, sparkling with fun, to delight conker fiends.

Tales from THE WIND IN THE WILLOWS
Kenneth Grahame

Episodes from the classic riverbank tales, carefully selected for the delight of younger readers. Wonderful illustrations by Margaret Gordon.

IT'S TOO FRIGHTENING FOR ME!
Shirley Hughes

Down by the railway a white face looks out of a spooky old house, and Jim and Arthur hardly dare investigate.

DINNER LADIES DON'T COUNT
Bernard Ashley

Two stories set in a school. Jason has to prove he didn't take Donna's birthday cards, and Linda tells a lie about why she can't go on the school outing.

MOULDY'S ORPHAN
Gillian Avery

Mouldy dreams of adopting an orphan, but when she brings one home to her crowded cottage, Mum and Dad aren't pleased at all.

THE TALE OF GREYFRIARS BOBBY
Virginia Derwent

A specially retold version for younger readers, of the true story of a scruffy Skye terrier who was faithful to his master even in death.